In memory of my mother, who loved cheeky monkeys

Monkey See, Monkey Do

Donough O' Malley

F

FRANCES LINCOLN
CHILDREN'S BOOKS

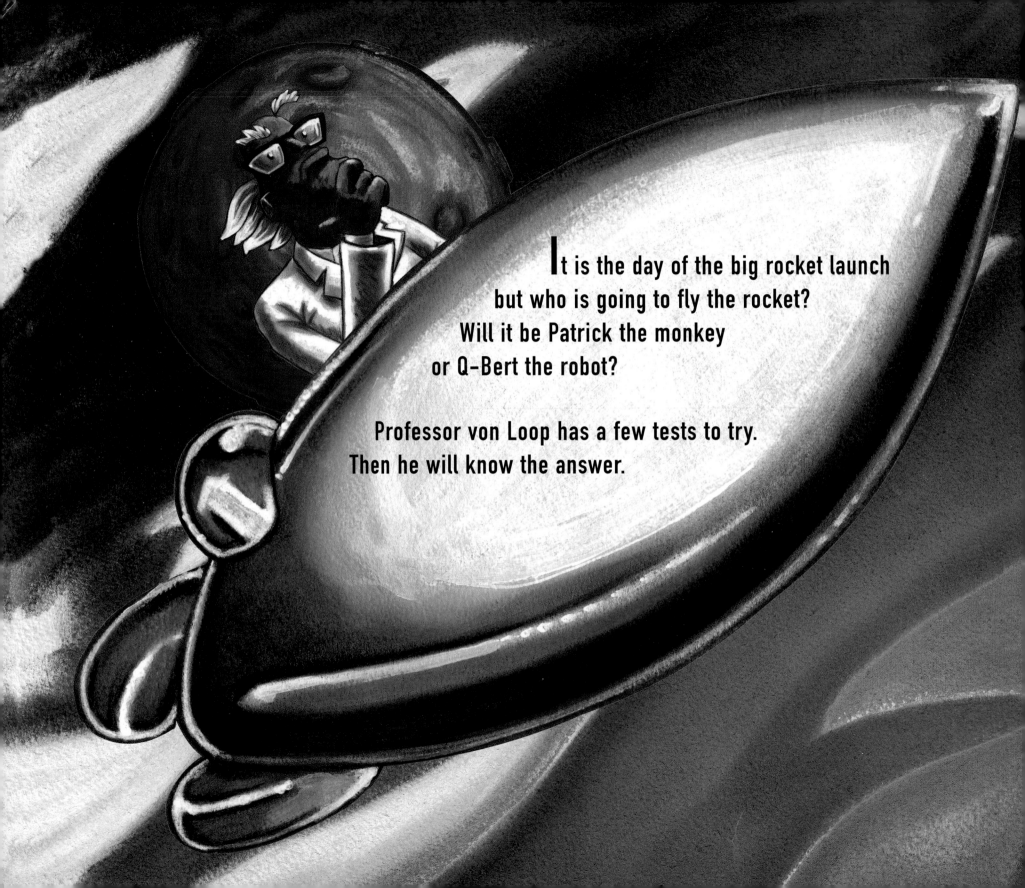

It is the day of the big rocket launch
but who is going to fly the rocket?
Will it be Patrick the monkey
or Q-Bert the robot?

Professor von Loop has a few tests to try.
Then he will know the answer.

First it's ... COUNTING.

What is 1+1?

Q-Bert writes a big clear 2.
But Patrick just does a big scribble.

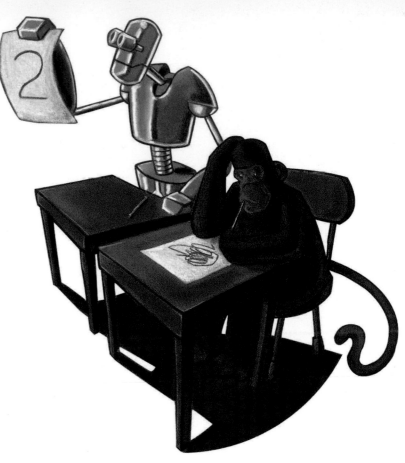

Next it's ... SHAKING HANDS.

Q-Bert gives the professor
a nice firm handshake.

But Patrick is downright rude!

Robot 2   Monkey 0

Then it's time for ...
BUILDING with blocks.

Q-Bert builds a pyramid.

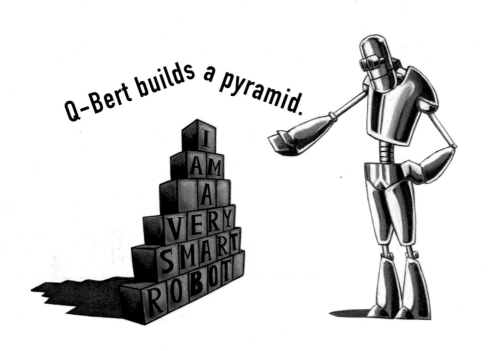

Patrick tries to eat his blocks.

"That monkey is not even trying," sighs Professor von Loop.

The last test is ...
DANCING.

Q-Bert dances like a robot ballerina.

But Patrick just falls on his bottom.

"Well, that decides it," says the professor. The robot flies this useless monkey back to his cage.

So with Patrick locked up tight the professor must hurry.
"I have to get ready for the launch," he says
as he turns off the light and closes the door.

In the dark, the only noise to be heard is the jangle of keys from Patrick's cage.

The door opens with a click and Patrick . . .

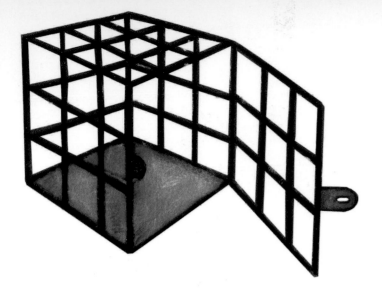

leaps out of the cage...

out of the window...

JUMP!

Outside is a tricycle
that Patrick borrows.

Patrick races towards the launch pad but there is a group of guards ready to stop anyone coming near the rocket.

They are no match for Patrick!

NO
MONKEYS

NO
ENTRY

SECURITY

As Patrick dances past the stumbling guards, he sees Q-Bert ready to blast off into the air.

Patrick doesn't have much time.
The countdown has begun.

"So," shouts Patrick, "who's useless now?
See you in 1000 light years!"